MW00975829

For my little, biddle babies

Little Bird
Biddle Bird

paintings & verse by David Kirk

SCHOLASTIC PRESS

CALLAWAY

NEW YORK

Little bird, Biddle bird,
Time for your snack.
But Mommy is busy
And hasn't come back.

Little bird, Biddle bird,
Mother has flown.
Is it time you were finding
Some food on your own?

Little bird, Biddle bird, What shall you eat?

Something squashy and salty?

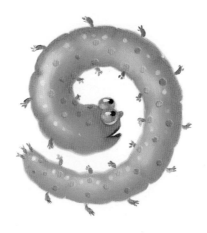

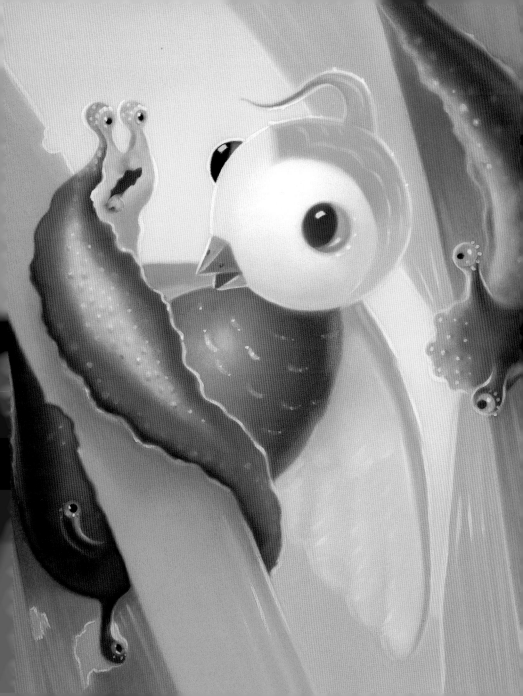

Or crunchy and sweet?

Little bird, Biddle bird,
Far from the nest,
How *can* a small bird know
What food tastes the best?

Is a flower a good meal?

Will a bug be a treat?

Don't gobble up tidbits
You find in the street!

Try not to peck things
That are too tough to chew,

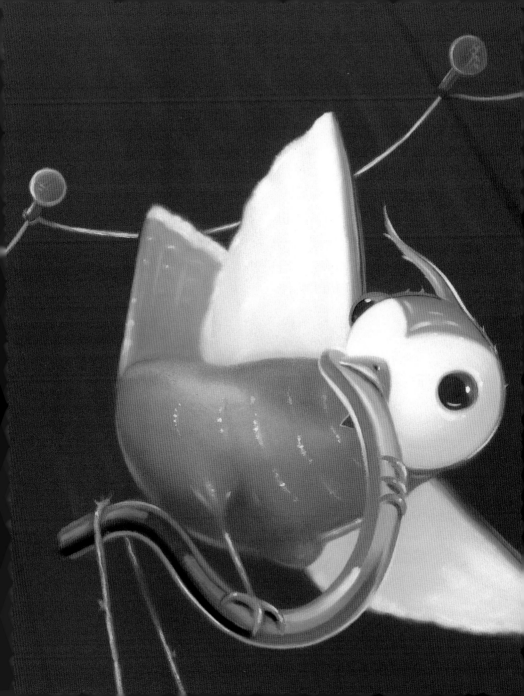

And never choose meals
That are bigger than you!

Little bird, Biddle bird,
You may be big,
But you won't catch that worm
If you aren't going to dig.

Little bird, Biddle bird,
Don't mess about —
Grab hold of that wormy
And wrestle him out!

Little bird, Biddle bird,
Full as can be —
Your proud mommy swoops
To your side from her tree.

Then all through the garden
Her voice can be heard,
Singing praise for her
Dear little big Biddle bird.

Nicholas Callaway, Editorial Director
Antoinette White, Senior Editor • Toshiya Masuda, Designer • True Sims, Production Director
Paula Litzky, Associate Publisher • Jeremy Ross, Director of New Technology • Roman Milisic, Assistant Editor
Ivan Wong, Jr. and José Rodríguez, Design and Production Associates
With thanks to Jennifer Braunstein at Scholastic Press and to Debbie Geri, Personal Assistant,
and Raphael Shea, Art Assistant, at David Kirk's studio.

Library of Congress catalog card number: 00-133492

ISBN 0-439-26092-2

10 9 8 7 6 5 4 3 2 1   01 02 03 04 05

Printed in Hong Kong by Palace Press International
First edition, March 2001

The paintings in this book are oils on paper.

THIS BIDDLE BOOK
BELONGS TO